USBORNE EASY READING

Tales from
Littletown

Felicity Brooks

Models by Jo Litchfield

Designed by Non Figg

Photography by Howard Allman
Edited by Jenny Tyler
Language consultant: Dr. Marlynne Grant Bsc, CertEd,
MEdPsych, PhD, AFBPs, CPsychol

Notes for parents

These stories have been written in a special way to help young children succeed in their first efforts to read.

Read each whole story aloud first, talking about the pictures as you go. Then encourage your child to read the short, simpler text at the top of each page and read the longer text underneath the pictures yourself. Taking turns with reading builds confidence and children do love joining in.

You can also help your child learn to recognize the important words from the stories by looking at the inside back cover where each word is shown next to its picture.

This delightful book provides an enjoyable way for parents and children to share the excitement of learning to read.

Managing designer: **Mary Cartwright** • Photographic manipulation: **John Russell**
Additional models: **Stefan Barnett**, **Les Pickstock**, **Barry Jones**, **Steven Lumley** and **Non Figg**

The Birthday Surprise

A story from Littletown

This is Polly and Jack Dot.

Here they are with Mr. Dot, Mrs. Dot and Pip the dog.

This is Littletown where they all live.

There is a little blue bird to find on every page

With thanks to **Eberhard Faber** for providing the **Fimo**® material for models and also to the **Model shop**, 151 City Road, London.

Polly, Jack and Mr. Dot go to the baker's.

Mr. Bun, the baker, has baked Polly a birthday cake.
Today is Polly's birthday.

The cake is in a big box.

"Let me see! Let me see!"
says Polly. "Not yet," says Mr. Dot. "It's a surprise."

Mr. Dot carries the cake.

"Have fun," calls Mr. Bun.
"Be careful with the cake!"

BUMP! "Be careful with
the cake!" says Mr. Dot.

CRASH! "Be careful with
the cake!" says Jack.

TRIP! "Be careful with
the cake!" says Polly.

Mr. Dot bumps the postman.
He almost drops the cake.

Mr. Dot slips on the road.
He almost drops the cake.

"The box is a little
squashed," says Jack.

"Were you careful with
the cake?" asks Mrs. Dot.

They take the cake into the kitchen.

Mrs. Dot takes off the ribbon.
Polly peeks inside the box.

It's a clown cake!

The clown has red hair, big shoes and a bow tie.

"What a wonderful cake!" says Polly. "I love clowns!"

Pip likes the look of the clown cake, too.

Pip jumps up and barks. Who's that at the door?

It's a real clown!

The clown has a big bag.
Pip sniffs his big shoes.

Polly is happy. She
shakes the clown's hand.

It's time for Polly's party.

Here are Polly's friends. They give her presents.
But where is the clown?

Up jumps the clown.

He pulls a tree out of his bag.

It grows and grows and grows.

He stands on one hand, makes balloon animals and juggles.

He is very funny.

He puts his hand
in his bag.

He pulls out a
pink pie.

Oh dear!
Now he trips.

SPLAT!

Everyone laughs, even the clown.

Polly blows out her candles.

It's time to eat. Polly likes her clown cake best.
"I'll give some to the real clown," she says.

But where is the clown?

He isn't under the table.

He isn't under the stairs.

He isn't behind the sofa.

And he isn't in the kitchen.

They can't find him anywhere.

It's time to go home.

Polly's friends say goodbye.
Polly wishes the clown had said goodbye too.

Polly goes outside to wave to her friends.

Out comes Mr. Bun. Polly is surprised to see him.
"I came to see if you were careful with the cake," he says.

Jack looks at Mr. Bun's bag.

I've seen that bag before.

"I think Mr. Bun was your birthday surprise," says Jack.
What do you think Jack means?

The Missing Cat

Another story from Littletown

This is Polly and Jack Dot.

Here they are with Mr. Dot, Mrs. Dot and Pip the dog.

This is Littletown where they all live.

There is a little blue bird to find on every page

Polly, Jack and Mrs. Dot are out shopping.

They are going to the butcher's shop to buy Pip a bone.

Mrs. Beef, the butcher, looks sad.

"My black cat, Oscar, is missing," she says.
"I'm going out to look for him."

"Can we look for Oscar too?" asks Polly.

"Just for a short while,"
says Mrs. Dot.

They ask the postman.
He hasn't seen a black cat.

They ask at the grocer's.
"There's no black cat here."

They ask at the market.
"There's no black cat here."

"Let's ask at the pet shop," says Polly.

But there's no one there to ask. "There's no black cat in there," says Jack. "Let's try the café."

21

They ask at the café.

"There are no black cats here."

"Look at these paw prints!" says Polly.

"Maybe Oscar made them," says Jack.
"Let's see where they go."

The paw prints go into the baker's shop.

"They are Pip's paw prints, not Oscar's," says Polly.
"Bad dog!" says Mrs. Dot.

Polly sees a black cat.

"Look," she says. "There's Oscar."
"He can't get down from the roof," says Jack.

Just then the fire truck comes by.

"Can I help?" asks Mr. Sparks, the fireman.
Polly points at the black cat. "Please rescue Oscar."

Mr. Sparks props up his ladder.

He climbs up the ladder.
"I'll save him," he says.

"Come on, Oscar. Don't
be frightened."

He carries the cat down
the ladder.

"Thank you," says Jack.
"Mrs. Beef will be pleased."

They take the cat to the butcher's shop.

But the shop is closed. "Mrs. Beef might be at home,"
says Mrs. Dot. "Let's go and see."

"Hello, Mrs. Beef. Here's Oscar," says Jack.

"That's not Oscar," says Mrs. Beef.

"This is Oscar. He was here when I came home."

"So who does this black cat belong to?" says Jack.

"I've no idea. It should go back where you found it."

Just then the cat jumps out of Jack's arms.

"You've found Missy!" cries Mrs. Bird from the pet shop.
"Thank you. I've been looking for her all day."

"Come and see Missy's new kittens."

Mrs. Bird leads the way to the pet shop. "We've seen lots of cats today," says Polly. "But I like dogs best," says Jack.

Here are some of Littletown's cats.

a fat cat,

a thin cat,

a lazy cat,

a big cat,

a tiny cat,

a striped cat,

a fluffy cat,

a smelly cat

and a grumpy cat.

Can you find them all?

The Runaway Orange

Yet another story from Littletown

This is Polly and Jack Dot.

Here they are with Mr. Dot, Mrs. Dot and Pip the dog.

This is a picture of Littletown where they live.

There is a little blue bird to find on every page

It's market day in Littletown.

Polly and Jack like the market. Pip likes the market too.
It's busy and noisy and there's lots to see.

Mrs. Dot is by the fruit stall.

Oops! She knocks an orange with her bag.
It falls from the stall. Can you see?

The orange rolls away.

Pip thinks it's a big, bouncy ball. He wants to play.
"Come back!" shouts Jack, but Pip doesn't stop.

Mrs. Bird's dogs join the fun.

They jump from her arms. "Come back, Tig!
Come back, Tag!" she cries, but the dogs don't stop.

The dogs chase the runaway orange.

They pass the fish stall.

They pass the cheese stall.

They pass the candy stall...

...and run along the road.

The dogs run into Mr. Bun, the baker.

He nearly drops his tray of cakes.
"Come back!" he shouts. But the dogs don't stop.

Now more dogs join the chase.

A black dog chases a big dog...

...who chases a small dog...

...who chases a puppy...

...who chases a spotted dog who chases...

They all run past the café.

There is a CRASH and a BANG, but the dogs don't stop.

They all race down the road.

They pass the butcher's.

They pass the post office.

They pass the bank...

...and pass the pet shop.

A boy kicks the orange.

The dogs stop! They watch the orange fly up in the air. Polly and Jack watch it too.

They chase the orange back up the road.

They pass the bank.

They pass the post office.

They pass the butcher's...

...back to the market!

Pip catches the runaway orange.

He drops it at Mrs. Dot's feet. "Bad dog, Pip," she says. "Look what you've done!"

Littletown is in a mess.

"Oh dear," says Jack. "Oh dear," says Polly.
"Oh dear," says Mrs. Dot.

"Who made this mess?" asks a policeman.

"Well, it all started with a runaway orange..." says Polly.
Can you remember what happened after that?

The words in these stories have been carefully chosen and often repeated to help develop your child's early reading skills. Here are some of the important words you will find in *The Birthday Surprise:*

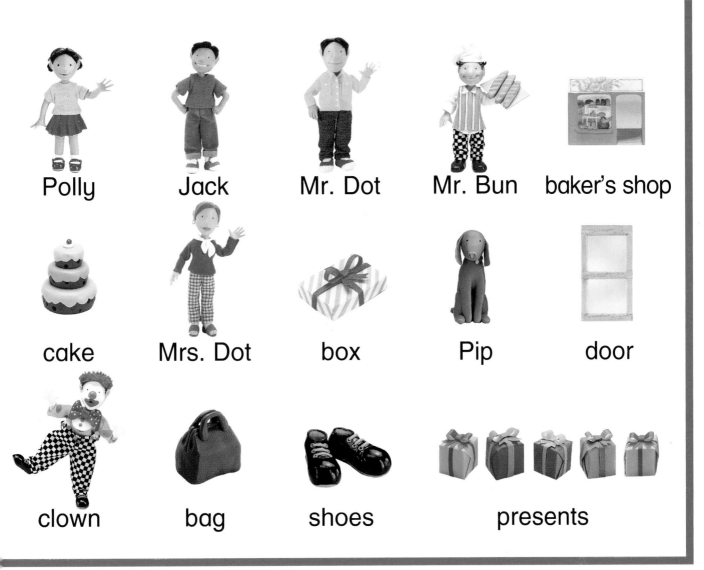

Polly

Jack

Mr. Dot

Mr. Bun

baker's shop

cake

Mrs. Dot

box

Pip

door

clown

bag

shoes

presents

The words for *The Missing Cat* and *The Runaway Orange* can be found on the next pages.

Here are some of the important words
you will find in *The Missing Cat:*

Polly   Jack   Mrs. Dot   shops

Pip   Mrs. Beef   black   cat   paw print

fire truck   fireman   ladder   Mrs. Bird